A Mea...
Life in the Flesh

By Craig Davidson

Rust and Bone

Craig Davidson

A Mean Utility and Life in the Flesh

PICADOR SHOTS

First published 2006 by Picador
an imprint of Pan Macmillan Ltd
Pan Macmillan, 20 New Wharf Road, London N1 9RR
Basingstoke and Oxford
Associated companies throughout the world
www.panmacmillan.com

ISBN-13: 978-0-330-44579-5
ISBN-10: 0-330-44579-0

1 3 5 7 9 8 6 4 2

A CIP catalogue record for this book is available from
the British Library.

Typeset by Intype Libra Ltd
Printed and bound in Great Britain by
Mackays of Chatham plc, Chatham, Kent

A Mean Utility

MIDWAY THROUGH THE PITCH I pass a note to Mitch Edmonds, big kahuna of graphic design: *This is going good?* He grimaces and scribbles back: *If by "good" you mean heart-stoppingly BAD, then yes, everything's PEACHY.* Diarrhetic adjective use aside, I suspect Edmonds is correct. In fact, the pitch is veering towards a crash of Hindenburg-like proportions: feel the heat of compressed helium flames and charred tatters of zeppelin silk buffeting my face, hear Herbert Morrison's breathless voice screaming "Oh the *humanity!*" into a giant wind-socked microphone.

Supp-Easy-Quit is a stop-smoking aid in suppository form. The science is sound: the rectal arterial clusters, feeding directly into the larger sacral and iliac branches, are ideal nicotine-delivery channels. Yet the stone-cold fact persists: most smokers—most *human beings*—exhibit a distinct disinclination to propel foreign objects up their bungs. They'd rather chew Nicorette until their mouths seize with lockjaw, festoon their bodies with the Patch, Christ, insert *flaming nicotine wedges* under their fingernails. This hard-wired predisposition renders the product a tough sell.

Don Fawkes, lead hand on the Supp-Easy-Quit account, aims a laser-pointer at a storyboard montage. "Okay," he says, "so here's this smoker who's trying to quit. He's in a smoky tavern—upscale, jazzy, bit of a speakeasy feel—tipping a few bevies, itching to fire off a lung rocket." Don believes his timely employment of hipster lingo is key to the middling success he enjoys. "So our man slips into the men's room and enters a stall, jazz music swells, he exits all smiles. Fade to black on the product logo."

The Supp-Easy-Quit reps—a power-suited Eva Braun flanked by a pair of lab-coated scientist pastiches—sit with arms crossed. The trio strike me as just-the-facts-ma'am types: their ideal commercial no doubt involves clinical footage of suppositories inserted into rectums, endoscopic cameras filming the dispersal of nicotine molecules into the bloodstream.

"Tell me: do you like it?" Don Fawkes, *Ignoramus extremus*, asks. "Do you *love* it?"

Fawkes's towering colossus of ineptitude fails to elicit any surprise or sympathy from me for two reasons: (1) last month Don single-handedly scuttled the Juicy Jubes kosher jujubes account, enraging a group of Hasidic entrepreneurs with the utterance of his ill-conceived tagline: *Juicy Jubes are Juicy JUI-licious!*; and (2) a large chunk of meat is missing from my left calf, a chunk roughly correspondent to the bite radius of a Rottweiler named Biscuits. The wound is cleaned and dressed but the calf is a fussy area, a locus of veins and connective tissues—blood seeps through the bandages, pooling in the heel of my Bruno Magli loafer.

I was mauled two nights ago, at a scratch-and-turn dogfight held in a foreclosed poultry processing plant outside Cobourg. Dottie, a three-year-old pit bull and my wife Alison's darling bitch, was matched uphill against a hard-biting presa canario named Chinaman. Dottie was a ten fight champ with heavily muscled stifles and a bite to shatter cinderblocks; Chinaman was cherry but his lineage legendary with chest and flews capable of deflecting bullets. Betting skewed in Dottie's favor on account of her experience and ring generalship.

After Alison gave Chinaman a thorough inspection—the breeder a jug-eared hillbilly known to soak his fighters' fur in poison—the dogs were led into a chicken-wire pen. White worms of chicken shit dotted the floor, some with downy feathers stuck to them. The concrete was puddled with blood from the previous fight.

Dottie started out fast, butting her muzzle into

Chinaman's chest and tearing a gaping hole above his right shoulder. Chinaman looked ready to buckle—it's the first critical injury that separates gamers from curs—but when Dottie went for his front leg he snapped at her skull, canines opening deep furrows across the bridge of her snout. Blood flowed down Dottie's chest and sprayed in her eyes. Alison gave a little moan. Chinaman's handler hollered, "Get at it, boy! Sic! *Sic!*"

The presa rushed hard and tried to pin Dottie against the pen. Dottie back-pedaled a few paces before fastening her mouth around Chinaman's advancing foreleg and ripping free a network of muscle and tissue. Chinaman kept pressing, chewing on Dottie's head; it sounded as if his teeth were raking bone. The crowd pressed around the pen, slapping the chicken-wire, stomping their feet. The smell was close and hot, sweetly animal.

The bell rang. Men with blunt baling hooks reached over the wire, digging into the dense muscling of the dogs' chests, prying them apart.

In the corner, I held Dottie while Alison went to work. After rubbing powdered Lidocaine into the dog's gumline to kill the pain, she chemically cauterized the facial wounds with ferric acid. Then she saturated a Q-tip with adrenaline chloride and swabbed the rims of Dottie's nostrils and ear holes, her anus. The dog's eyes, previously glazed, attained a clear focus.

The bell rang. Both dogs scratched the chalk line.

Dottie lived up to her reputation as a wrecker in the second. She butted hard into Chinaman's stifles, attacking that shoulder wound. Chinaman gave as good as he got, slashing at Dottie's dewlap, shredding it. At the eight-minute mark: a fibrous *snap* as Chinaman's shoulder broke. The presa was down to three legs. Dottie pressed her advantage, forcing Chinaman back, attacking the throat, a blur of snapping teeth, questing jaws, and bloody ropes of saliva as each dog angled for the killing clinch.

Chinaman managed to close his mouth around

Dottie's muzzle, gripping her entire upper palate. The brittle splintering sound was unlike anything I'd ever heard. Dottie's spine stiffened and her claws tore at Chinaman's belly.

The bell rang. An acne-scarred teenager mopped up blood and redrew the chalk line.

Dottie's face was in ruins: bloody and cleaved open, shards of bone free-floating beneath the skin. Half her nose was torn off and her dewlap hung like tattered curtains. Alison debrided the worst wounds with hydrogen peroxide and Betadine before slicking them with mixed adrenaline and Vaseline.

"Pick your dogs up!" a man hollered. "That's enough. Enough!" The crowd jeered him.

"Maybe I should," Alison said. "Pick her up."

I'd've rather cut my foot off and eaten it! "Look at that one," I said with a nod at the presa, who was burrowing his head in the breeder's chest like it wanted to climb inside and die. "Bet you a steak dinner it doesn't toe the scratch."

Chinaman's breeder grabbed the dog by its

neck and whipsawed it back and forth, growling, "Don't flake on me, you goddamn cur. Don't you fucking *flake*."

Before the bell Alison injected 10 cc's Epinephrine into Dottie's haunch. I felt the dog's fluttering heart rate normalize. Chinaman staggered from his corner, front right leg limp as a cooked noodle. The presa's muzzle was frosted white with Lidocaine.

Round three ended it. Dottie feinted at Chinaman's bum leg off the scratch and, in one deft move, rammed her skull into his good one. Forced to support his entire forward weight, Chinaman's left foreleg snapped. The presa toppled face-first, front legs splayed to either side, hinds scrabbling feebly. Dottie started clawing at Chinaman's eyes. Before long the baling hooks pulled her off.

After squaring all bets I was lugging Dottie through the parking lot—blood saturating her doggie blanket, dripping through the kennel crate's metal honeycombs—when this raspy barking kicked up from behind. I wheeled to see a huge Rottweiler bullrushing my blind side. It wore an inch-thick studded leather collar against which the striated muscle of its throat and neck pulsed. Links of twenty-gauge chain spat gravel between its legs.

I dropped Dottie and fired an off-balance kick. The rottie passed under my leg, clamping down on my calf.

Events unfolded at the narcotic pace of a fugue. My right knee buckled and I went down, blacktopped gravel dimpling the ass of my cotton Dockers. My skull caromed off the ground and everything whited out for a moment. Then I was struggling up, fists beating a frenzied tattoo on the dog's head as its square dark muzzle worried into the wound. Dottie pressed her busted face to the kennel's grate, growling low in her throat, bloody bubbles forced between her black eyes and orbital bone. The Rottweiler wrenched its head sideways, teeth sunk deep into the sinews of my calf, gator-rolling me across that chill November tarmac.

Five sausage-link digits grasped the underside of the rottie's jaw, thumb and index finger pressed to the axis where upper and lower palate met, forcing the mouth open. The woman restraining the animal was an eclipse of flesh clad in what appeared to be a pleated topsail, calves thick as an adolescent pachyderm's networked with bluish spider veins. A slimly ironic menthol cigarette hung off her bottom lip, defying all known laws of gravity.

"Bad Biscuits," she chastised the dog in a breathy baby-voice. "The manners on you. Why you want to go biting the nice man?"

Alison arrived in a blur of shawls and indignation. I noticed she poked her fingers through Dottie's crate before arriving at my side. Bright arterial blood pumped from my calf.

"Stop squirming," she told me, breaking out the peroxide and catgut to attend to the wound.

The woman waddled to her idling Cutlass

Supreme. She opened the driver's door—sun-blistered dashboard lined with neon-haired Treasure Trolls; bingo dabbers spilling from a sprung glovebox—swatting the dog inside. A shrewish, stoop-shouldered man sat in the passenger's seat, wearing camouflage fatigue pants and the kind of sleeveless white T-shirt favored by aged Italian gardeners.

"You can't," I said, reaching out to her. "Can't just . . . your dog *bit me!*"

She tucked her chin to her chest, setting in motion a rippling domino-effect of subsidiary chins. "Biscuits got a touch of the ringworm, misser. Gives him the cranks." Her look suggested I wasn't much of a dogman if I didn't know *that*. "Every one my babies is papered and rabies free. Don't need shots, promise."

"That dog should be destroyed!"

"I'm'n a *pretend* I didn't *hear* that, misser."

She jerked the door shut and fishtailed down the row of diagonally parked cars. Biscuits hurled his body at the Cutlass's rear window, barking wrathfully, white froth slathering the glass.

"Did that woman just . . .?"

"Yes," Alison palmed me a vitamin K tablet to promote blood clotting. "Let's go."

"But you can't—"

"What do we tell the cops?" she said. "We were at this illegal dogfight and . . ."

"But we live in a polite society!" I was raving by now. "We operate under civilized rules!"

"Hush."

"I should bite *her*—bite that gargantuan . . . *ASS!*"

"Hush."

Halfway home Alison pulled off the highway. Dottie was emitting low wheezing sounds from the back seat, thrashing on the blood-thick blanket and tearing her stitches open.

We wrangled the kennel crate onto the rough shale of the breakdown lane. In the dead white of an arc-sodium streetlight I broke the kennel down, there being no other way to get her out.

Alison held the dog's square head in her hands, massaging the neck and stomach, anywhere not gored. The medicinal smell of Epinephrine seeped out of Dottie's many cuts.

"Oh, Jesus. I can't bury another dog, Jay."

Alison touched Dottie's head, tracing her fingertips along the muzzle, kneading the expanse of slick fur between the ears. The dog looked up with sad, grateful eyes. Crickets chirped in long reeds bordering the ditch.

Near the end Alison injected Lidocaine into Dottie's temple, between the ring and index fingers on my left hand, which were cupped over the dog's tight-lidded eyes. Cars moved past on the highway, bathing our bodies in headlight glow. Dottie vomited blood. Her eyelids fluttered against my palm.

"I should've picked her up."

The dog started shaking then, the convulsions wracking her bones, radiating outwards.

"She wouldn't allow it," I said. "Dottie was a deep game dog."

"Are you loving it?" Don Fawkes repeats for the umpteenth time. "Tell me you love it."

But the Supp-Easy-Quit reps are clearly *not* loving it, a fact Helen Keller could've gleaned, but of which Fawkes remains blissfully unaware. Eva Braun jots in a faux-calfskin dossier with aggressive, slashing cursive while her lab-coated bookends eye Fawkes as they might a particularly offensive strain of bacterium smeared across a specimen slide.

Mitch Edmonds passes me a doodle: some guy with a gourd-shaped head in which a candle burns jack-o-lantern style, one eye twice outsizing the other, pumpkintoothed and drooling, squiggly stink-lines and bowtie flies and a speech bubble reading: *You love it! You really, really love it!*

Dr. Clive Ketchum's fertility clinic is located in a neocolonial-style office building at the corner of Steeles and Yonge. I mount the steps leading up to a narrow hallway with hesitancy. Took a Xanax at lunch, another on the cab ride over—feeling *no* pain.

Ketchum's waiting area resembles a film noir movie set: a large, dim, oak-paneled room with high ceiling, frosted-glass valances, a white sand ashtray under a no-smoking sign. The receptionist is young, petite, and blond, with prominent tits and an air of having woken this morning knowing in advance every move she'd make for the remainder of the day.

"I have the five o'clock."

She consults the appointment book. "Mr. James Paris?"

I tip her a wink, resisting—barely—the urge to flex.

She leads me down a well-lit corridor into a spare antiseptic room. She gestures to an examination table and orders me to strip to my skivs before excusing herself.

I hoist myself onto the examination table. Butcher paper crinkles under my thighs. A large medical illustration adorns the opposite wall:

Scrotum and Contents. It's all there: the superficial and external spermatic fascias, the tunica vaginalis, the epididymis and the testes, which, in this artist's rendition, resemble capillary-threaded quail's eggs. Disembodied tweezer-tips pinch and peel back to reveal strata of flesh and membrane and nerve.

Dr. Ketchum enters. The man's dimensions are those of a bowling pin, the majority of weight distributed to the hindquarters, and yet his body remains somehow insubstantial, as if stuffed with wadded newspapers.

He flips open a dossier, nodding, then shaking his head. "You've been doing the exercises?" He performs a series of spread-legged knee bends, arms veed in front of him like a high diver. Ketchum contends this maneuver—the "gonad agitator"—will promote sperm production and, in tandem with other, uniformly unpleasant exercises—the "urethral tube widener," the "scrotal exciter"—will have me shooting live rounds in no time.

"I've been doing them."

"It's strange."

"What?"

"Strange your sperm count hasn't increased since the start of your exercise regimen." He gives me a look. "It is my experience that men tend to baby their testes, usually as a result of early childhood trauma. But believe me when I say they're terrifically hardy organs. My advice is to really push yourself. Make those testicles *work* for you. Give them hell, as it were."

"I've been giving them . . . hell."

"Is that so?"

"It's been . . . a regular boot camp."

Dr. Ketchum chuckles perfunctorily. "Alright. The problem remains, James. Your scrotal sac is simply too *hot*. A blast furnace in there."

This is not new information. Five years ago, when our fledgling, lighthearted attempts at conception ended in failure, we blamed our lack of success on job stress, our recent relocation, a sheer lack of dedication to the task at hand. But as the streak lengthened, the finger of blame began to point wildly: the moon's cycles/Alison's low-protein diet/my pack-a-day habit/malevolent otherworldly forces. Alison visited a fertility clinic and, through a non-invasive, airy-fairy, casting-of-bones procedure I never truly understood, her womb was given a clean bill of health. Confusion and guilt propelled me to Dr. Ketchum's office, where a violently invasive, teeth-clenchingly painful process disclosed that my scrotum's core temperature equaled that of a steam cooker's. The few vulcanized sperm able to withstand the heat were reduced to heaving their exhausted flagellate forms against my wife's egg in the manner of bedraggled boat-people flinging themselves upon the impregnable walls of an asylum-denying nation.

Ketchum prescribed pills and herbal remedies, ordered the daubing of foul-smelling ointments and the quaffing of putrid teas. He suggested immersion in cold baths or icepack application to the affected region before intercourse. None of these measures proving effective, Ketchum advocated a strenuous exercise routine and . . . other tactics.

"Have you encouraged your wife to stimulate you anally? Gentle manipulation of the sphincter encourages more vigorous orgasms and promotes semen—"

"No, we . . . no."

Ketchum emits a robust, let's-not-be-prudish laugh. "Then by all means *try*. It's a natural, healthy sexual activity. Nothing peculiar or unmanly about it."

A fleeting image: Ketchum's naked, pinata-hollow body squirming delightedly under the anal ministrations of a faceless, tentacle-fingered woman.

"It's not that desperate."

"But your wife must be getting impatient."

"Alison's fine," I lie.

Sex has become a grim struggle punctuated by bizarre and superstitious rituals. While I lounge in bed with a bag of frozen peas thawing in my boxers, Alison discreetly checks her internal temperature against the magical twenty-seven degrees Centigrade ideal for conception. She has dressed as a French maid, a succubus, a cheerleader—*Ra-ra, hey-hey, fertilize that egg today!*—a schoolgirl, a milkmaid; the local costume shop conducts a brisk trade on my singular shortcoming. No sooner have I made my contribution than she's shoved me away, elevating her hips and bicycle-kicking her legs, body contorted into grotesque runic formations to aid my seed in "taking." Worst is the look on Alison's face as I come: a look of disquieting, anxious futility. *Not this time, tiger. You didn't bring the thunder.*

"Alison's just fine," I repeat. "We have other interests."

"Wonderful. It's important for couples with such issues to pursue outside goals." He flips the dossier shut. "Keep those exercises up—" a few more demonstrative deep-knee bends "—and don't forget the urethra-widening—" his eyes trail down to my calf "—good lord, James, what happened to your leg?"

Alison's father owns a dairy farm on the outskirts of St. Catharines. When he spies a sick cow, he spraypaints an orange circle around the rear left leg. At night, when all the other chores are finished, he leads it to a brook running behind the house and shoots it in the skull. Once, when Alison and I were visiting at Christmas, he asked her to take care of a sick calf; it was cold and her father's arthritis was acting up. Alison asked did he keep his gun in the same spot.

Bundled in parkas and toques, we went out to the barn. Can't say why I tagged along, exactly, except perhaps morbid curiosity, or out of the misplaced notion she needed the moral support. The barn was dark and earthy, claustrophobic with the stink of livestock. Cattle snorted and heaved, expelling plumes of oyster-gray steam from their nostrils. We waded between their milling flanks, guided by bars of dusky sunlight pouring through the slats. A sponge-like tumor the rough size of a softball was tethered to the calf's jaw by a strip of skin. Alison shooed the youngster from its hiding spot beneath its mother's belly. The cow let it go without a fight, as if knowing it was sick, what needed to be done.

She led it down to the water, guiding it gently with a switch snapped off an elm tree. The calf's eyes wide and dark and dumb. The grotesque tumor bump-bumped against its throat. Early twilight hung suspended over the fields, patches of orange burning between the trees. Sparrows clustered on a snow-topped log lying in the middle of the brook.

Alison settled the shotgun against the calf's head. It flicked its ear, as though the muzzle were a fly it wished to shoo. I remember wind whistling down my neck and feeling terribly cold.

Alison cocked the hammer and calmly pulled the trigger. The gunshot was louder than I expected, a rough bark rolling out across the clean snow-topped expanse. The animal went down silently. It half-stood on its front legs. The left side of its face was just . . . *gone*, I wanted to yell "Go down, just go *down*," the way a trainer would to an overmatched boxer. It fell over on its side in the shallows. We went back inside for hot toddies.

Half an hour after my doctor's appointment, I step through the front door of our house. From the upstairs nursery arises the plaintive clamor of pit bull puppies seeking attention—attention I studiously deny. Pass down a hallway hung with photos of champion pits chained to spikes pounded into browned patches of grass, mouths open and teeth bared, straining against their fetters.

Alison stands over the kitchen sink shaking water from a colander of diced zucchini. The cordless telephone is cinched between her shoulder and ear.

"No, no," she's saying, her tone that of a mother explaining a crucial fact to a particularly dimwitted child, "that is *not* the progression. Bulldog to German shepherd to Doberman pinscher to Rottweiler to pit bull. It goes *no further*. There is no evolution."

I place my hands on her hips and bring them around, fingers knitting over her bellybutton.

"No, I don't . . . no . . . that's in-*sane*." She twists out of my grasp, pressing the mouthpiece directly to her lips, as if this forced intimacy will convey the truth of her argument. "The presa canario is nothing more than a puffed-up bully. I mean, will a hundred-twenty-pound presa beat a pit? In all probability, yes. But a heavyweight boxer would pummel a flyweight—it's no contest. That's why there's weight classes . . . no . . . alright, yes . . . listen, I'm not going to argue." Alison hangs her tongue out. "Fine, if that's how you see it. All I'll say is, pound for pound, nothing beats a pit. *Pound* for *pound*, yes . . . okay . . . fine . . . we agree to disagree."

She jams the phone in its charging cradle and blows a raspberry at it.

"Who?"

"Nobody. Nothing. How was work?"

"Fawkes deep-sixed the Supp-Easy-Quit account."

"It's a tough product to market."

Alison always lets Fawkes off the hook. I took her to the office Christmas party last year and discovered the two of them in the copy room, sloppy drunk and giggling, photocopying asexual body parts: elbows, fingers, wrists, foreheads.

"And your day?"

"Oh, Dr. Scalise was being Dr. Scalise." Dr. Phillip Scalise, the cardiovascular surgeon at North York General, is thirty-five with the coarse-skinned face and dimpled chin of a *Look Who's Talking*–era John Travolta. Alison is his "all-time favorite" OR nurse. "During prep he was telling these awful jokes, just plain *awful*, and I shouldn't have been laughing but he's really just so silly sometimes."

I recognize this should bother me but, doubtlessly due to the Xanax I popped on the homebound subway, I find myself supremely non-plussed. "He's a silly one," I agree. "I'll go feed the dogs."

The sky's an odd color: a deep but muted red, the color of diluted grenadine. Someone a few houses over is doing yardwork: the staccato *chop-chop-chop* of a lawnmower rises above the pines. The training shed is set into the far left corner in the shade of a leafless maple. The maple is four feet wide at its base, thick lower limbs jutting almost parallel to the ground. I've often imagined nailing split two-by-twos into the trunk, a stepladder up to the boughs capable of supporting weight. I'd lay down planks and erect sturdy retaining walls, a corrugated-tin roof for rainy days, a rope-and-bucket dumbwaiter, maybe even a walkie-talkie link allowing for communication during those first nights of independence.

The shed is of solid prewar construction, dirt floor spread with Bardahl to keep the dust down. I take down a pair of ballistic-nylon gloves from a nail pounded into the doorframe and scoop Iam's Science Diet into steel tureens.

The chicken-wire pens house three fighters but now Dottie's gone we're down to a pair. Rodney is a four-year-old male, forty-seven pounds of bone and sinew and teeth, winner of five consecutive, most recently the first-round butchery of Grand Chief Negrino, a vastly overrated Neapolitan mastiff bitch. I set the tureen in front of him and, while he eats, first gently but with increasing force, punch the crown of his skull until he snaps viciously at my gloved hand.

"Good boy."

Matilda is the most aggressive fighter I've ever raised. Her nose is pressed to the chicken-wire, snuffling. She has a short, clean brindle coat with a pattern of gray stripes over a base coat of jet black. I stroke her sleek head and boxy muzzle, running a fingertip across the crescent-moon scars left after her ears were amputated. She licks the glove with her large pink tongue.

I slap her as hard as I can.

The blow doesn't budge her and then teeth flash, dense muscling of chest and flews flexes, jaws seize the glove in a bone-splintering grip and shake so violently it seems my shoulder will be jerked from socket.

"Mat—aark! *Aaaagh!*"

I manage to drop the tureen inside her pen. Matilda immediately releases me and pads over to the kibble. I am struck, as I so often am, by the unstudied perfection of these animals.

Pit bulls are utterly fearless. It is a reckless, lunatic sort of fearlessness, a fearlessness suggesting the breed lacks any true conception of that emotion. Beauty exists in that fearlessness, and so the breed itself is beautiful. It is beautiful to watch your pit toe the scratch against a dog twice its size and note, in its posture and its eyes, the flat and unflinching assurance of victory. It is beautiful to hold a pit's wine-cask body between rounds, to take in its hideous wounds—ears bitten off and eyes crushed from orbit, compound-fractured legs, flesh stripped to the bone—and see nothing but a cold resiliency, an *eagerness*. These dogs truly believe they are invincible. They believe they will never die. It is beautiful to watch two pits at the end of a hard roll, lying in the pen's center or pressed up against the wire, slick with blood, blind and exhausted, licking one another with a shocking tenderness. The simple fact of their existence is its own beauty: there are creatures on this Earth upon whom the human frailties of pain, weakness, self-doubt exert no bearing.

Alison and I talk about our mutual fascination. Lately, it's about the only topic that doesn't lead to an argument. Sometimes she'll ask the question: *Should we be doing this?* I look at it like boxing: you train your fighter to the best of your ability, bring him along slowly, don't put him in against a murderer. "Besides," I tell her, "these dogs want to fight. They can't vocalize it, sure, but you can see, I can see. It's what they *do*." She'll nod slightly, say, "The way herding is what a sheepdog does, huh?" in a small voice that doesn't quite seem to believe. "Ex-*actly*, dear."

I walk back to the kitchen. The combined pain of my leg (Biscuits) and shoulder (Matilda) compounded by the ambient soreness resulting from ten minutes of urethral widening exercises has killed the Xanax buzz. I pull two T-bone steaks from the deep-freeze and set them on the counter to thaw. Then I retrieve bottles of rum and Creme de Banane from the cupboard, eyeball shots into a pair of wide-mouthed highball glasses, top them off with heavy cream.

Alison's in the nursery. Walls painted bright yellow, hardwood floor spread with sections of the *Globe and Mail*. Two mobiles: tinfoil baseball players shagging fly balls; tinfoil ballerinas pirouetting endlessly. A molded plastic chair with a dog-eared copy of Sun Tzu's *The Art of War* resting upon it, from which I often quote passages to the dogs: *In peace prepare for war, in war prepare for peace . . .*

My wife on the floor, surrounded by pups.

They paw her in clumsy, exploratory fashion, climbing over her hips and breasts, capturing her shirt collar between their teeth and shaking their oversize puppy heads. I sit on pissy newspapers and offer her a glass.

"How was your appointment?" she says.

"Some different exercises."

Alison sets her glass down. A puppy commences licking the beaded condensation. "I was talking to someone at work," she says, "about artificial insemination. Interesting option—leaf through a donor book, choose a suitable candidate."

I imagine a houseful of miniature John Travoltas, or, worse yet, Don Fawkeses, running up and down the halls, sticky-fingered and greasy-haired, telling silly-awful jokes and asking if I love them. "I don't think we need to explore that option."

"I'm thirty-three, Jay," she persists. "Conception after thirty-five is basically a no-go."

A pup noses the toe of my loafer. I give it a

boot, sending it skittering across the floor. "I'm thinking about scheduling a roll for Matilda."

"A roll? Now?"

I set my empty glass down and pick Alison's up.

"Mattie's barely a yearling," she says. "You haven't worked her properly . . ."

"She's the strongest dog I've ever seen. She'll crucify anybody."

"There's not an even-weight dog on the circuit she could be rolled against."

"I'd be matching her uphill."

"By how many pounds? Against *who*?"

I raise her glass to my lips. Our eyes meet over the rim.

"No way," she says with dawning awareness. "The Rottweiler that bit you is double her weight."

"Matilda will eat that mutt up. Devour him."

Alison cradles a puppy in her arms, kneading its baggy skin between her fingers.

"Stop coddling," I tell her. "Make a cur out of it."

The puppy takes her finger in its mouth, gnawing, slobbering. "Matilda's not ready."

"She'll . . . whup him."

"Roll with Rodney, at least."

"Matilda's ready."

She stands and walks to the window. With the night pressed against the window glass, the darkness reflects her face set in rigid lines. Alison doesn't have the sort of features that become more attractive with anger, the high Latin cheekbones or bee-stung lips that, when flushed, evoke a certain male stirring. She is much prettier when calm and accommodating.

"Matilda didn't bite you. It's not her fault."

"That's not what this is about!" I sway unsteadily to my feet, chest puffed with righteous indignation. The glass slips from my grasp and shatters on the floorboards. Puppies rush at the yellow mess. I kick at them, "Watch the broken glass, you little shits!"

Alison gathers double handfuls of newspaper and sops the spill. She's ditched the OR scrubs for a paint-flecked crop-topped shirt and a pair of cutoffs—her "bumming around gear," which she knows I find sexy in a slovenly, hausfrau-ish way. Her hair is combed out in feathered waves that I'd like to plunge my hands and face into. Her face seems suddenly pretty again, the face of the woman I married.

"Honey. Listen." I lick my lips and try to straighten my tie before realizing I'm no longer wearing one. "You know what? Hey, what—*hey*, what the hell was I thinking?" I'm in the boardroom, wheeling and dealing, soothing bruised egos, smoothing things over. "Matilda's not ready. You're absolutely right." Sell it, baby. *Sell it!* "We'll wait, okay? We'll just wait."

Her features soften into something approaching belief. "I think it's for the best . . ."

"Sure. Sure, I think so." I kneel beside her, picking up shards of glass. This triggers the discomforting memory of a fight we had months ago, a fight over . . . what? Finances, booze, assumed infidelities. The usual suspects. As the fight crested towards its predictable apex, I'd stormed into the den, plucked a blown-glass globe from the mantel—a gift from that honey-dripping bastard Dr. Scalise, bartered from a legless peddler in Malta—and hurled it into the fireplace, where it exploded with a brittle tinkling sound.

"It's a good decision," she says.

"Sure."

"You think?"

"Sure I think."

Sometime that night, after a bout of energetic but futile congress, I have a dream. In this dream, I stand stark naked in the middle of a cavernous auditorium. The tiered stands are packed. Not with people—birds. Bluebills and meadowlarks, flamingoes and penguins, turkey vultures, toucans, sandpipers, pelicans, even a dodo. The sounds they make are disquieting: feathers rustling, talons scrabbling, beaks digging ticks from molting plumage. The aviary smell of them—dust and millet and caked shit—clogs my nostrils. I clear my throat, unsure of how to address this throng, yet convinced it is expected of me. Beady dark eyes, thousands of them, stare down.

"I'm sure you're wondering why I've called this meeting . . ."

Then my penis falls off. Not just my cock: balls, ball sack, pubes. The whole apparatus. My tackle doesn't drop so much as *float* to the ground in a series of oscillating parabolas, light as tissue paper, settling gently on the concrete. Touch my plucked groin with a trembling hand. The skin is pebbled, like the rind of an orange.

Every bird in the auditorium takes flight; the sound of their wings fills my ears like a stiff, storm-bearing wind. They swoop down, the flurry of their beating wings messing my meticulously styled hairdo. White gobs of guano pelt my face and chest. An army of birds descend upon my penis. I squawk, a birdlike sound, pushing through the feathery mob to recover it. A thousand beaks pecking, two thousand clawed feet raking, air thick with feathers. "That's mine!" I scream. A yellow goose with Xanax eyes hisses and bites at my fingers. A hummingbird with Tippi Hedren's face flies up my nose, flitting about behind my eyes. "No!" I scream pitifully. "I *need* that!"

The birds take flight *en masse*, flying up through a hole in the auditorium ceiling, vanishing into the vast pewter sky. Apart from the downy drifts of tail feathers, the floor is bare.

A black smudge marks the cement approaching the processing plant's loading bay doors. Years ago, after his Doberman bitch dropped a brutal roll to a wrecking-ball presa canario, some owner doused his dog with kerosene and set it on fire. The Doberman, leg-broke and missing skin from its face and haunches, ran in herky-jerk circles, biting at the flames climbing down her throat and igniting her lungs. She lay down, then lay still as a stone and burned to blackness on the concrete.

I step over the smudge and into the warehouse. Matilda's crate hangs at the end of my left arm, the dog dozing inside. Alison trails behind, lugging a diaper bag packed with narcotics, needles, catgut, gauze. She's here solely for Mattie's sake.

The morning after my bird dream, I told Alison in no uncertain terms that Matilda would be fighting Biscuits as soon as it could be arranged. She stared at me, toothbrush jutting from her mouth, lips frothy with paste. She shook her head, "I should have known." I said, "Hey, Mattie will kill that rottie!" and pinched the pudge girding her waistline. She slapped my hand away with a closed fist, called me a name. *Bastard? Fucker?* Her mouth was full of toothpaste.

Unaware of her opponent's trainer, the fat hillbilly—Lola Snape, the matchmaker told me—agreed to match Biscuits against Matilda. I wade through a crowd of dogmen, gawkers, and fight bums to the weigh-in. One guy wears a Russian fur hat and an electric-blue seersucker suit with hand-sewn bolts of red-and-purple lightning down each sleeve. He heels, on a shoestring leash, a peanut-sized pomeranian with a streak of red-dyed fur running skull to tail-tip.

Lola and her husband wait at the scale. She appraises me for a good twenty seconds before a flicker of recognition crosses her cow eyes.

"How's that leg, misser?" She pronounces leg as *laig*.

The weighmaster sets Matilda's crate on the scale. After subtracting fifteen pounds for the kennel, Matilda's official weight is fifty-three pounds.

I clip a lead onto Matilda's collar and draw her from the crate. Her body is a canine anatomy chart, every tendon group and connective ligature clearly visible beneath a thin sheath of skin. Her legs are roped with thickly dilated veins. She squats on her haunches and scratches behind her left ear, gaze never leaving the hulking rottie.

Biscuits tips the scale at a buttery ninety-three pounds. I am heartened to see his pendulous gut and bony forelegs, deficiencies I failed to note on our first encounter. His back and flanks are deeply scarred where he's been bitten, or more likely beaten. He growls at Matilda, upper lip rippling to expose canines the size and color of large cashews.

Their weights are chalked on a tote board, next to their records—Biscuits a surprising 11–1. The line is established at 3–1 against Matilda on account of her weight, greenhorn status, and murky lineage. The line excites a good deal of betting.

As we lead our dogs to the pen, Lola leans over and says, "Fat chance your little yapper's gonna beat my Biscuits." Days later, lying bandaged and in a hospital bed, a late-blossoming riposte of Churchillian wit will come to me—*You, madam, are the fattest chance I've ever laid eyes on*—but at the moment I simply entreat her to fuck off. She looks to her haystack-haired hubby in hopes he'll defend her honor, but the weevil-legged woodhick is engrossed by his gumboots.

"It'll be alright," I tell Alison, assuming she's noticed Biscuits's shortcomings.

"Whatever."

"Matilda will demolish him."

"Whatever."

We usher our dogs into the pen. I've got hold of Matilda's scruff over the chicken-wire; her body thrums like a high-tension powerline. A dwarfish man with phony hair rings the bell for round one.

The rottie comes out strong, thinking Matilda will be easy to stop in the first round, only Matilda isn't there. She feints left on Biscuits's lead-off charge, ducks under his advancing left foreleg, fastens onto the hanging meat of his abdomen. The bigger dog back-pedals madly, yelping, biting down at Matilda's thrashing head.

Lola hollering, "Get that little shit! Bite her! Get off, *get off*!"

The rottie twists his body sideways and Matilda tumbles across the pen with a chunk of Biscuits in her mouth. A rude bloody hole in the rottie's gut but he's still very much game.

The dogs square around as the crowd clusters close to the pen, leaning in for better views. Biscuits steps from left foreleg to right, then right to left, a boxer's shuffle. Matilda stands stock-still, mouth open, haunches quivering.

The rottie rushes again, crouched low, head tucked. Flashing teeth tear his ear to shreds before he smashes into Matilda's stifles, barreling her into the chicken-wire. Alison pokes her fingers through the wire, fingers clenched. Biscuits has Matilda pressed against the pen—Matilda pivots, lashing out with her hind legs, aiming for the gut-wound. Jaws come together, two or three splintered teeth skittering across the ground. With a level of cunning I wouldn't have guessed at, Biscuits fakes a strike at Matilda's throat, reverses and bites down on the rear right haunch. Matilda emits a shrill yowl.

"That's it, boy! Get at her!"

Teeth sunk deep into Matilda's flank, Biscuits drags her away from the chicken-wire. Matilda's body whips side to side, paws scrabbling uselessly. Alison's grip on the wire tightens as Biscuits shakes his head, neck tendons bunching. Blood pours down Matilda's brindled coat.

The bell rings. Men reach over the pen with blunted baling hooks to pry the dogs apart.

Matilda trots stiffly to the corner, rear right leg tucked close to her chest. I snap a muzzle on and grip her barrel chest as Alison goes to work. "Easy, Mattie baby," Alison whispers to the squirming dog.

She cleans away the blood and debrides the cuts with a mixture of hydrogen peroxide and rubbing alcohol. Peering down through the layers of meat, she winces.

"Severed veins."

"Do what you do."

After swabbing the deep tissues with a thick coagulant, she sprays the topmost layers with Granulex. Then she spreads the wounds' lips and cauterizes them with ferric acid. Matilda squeals against her muzzle. I glance at the other corner, where Lola runs a bead of Crazy Glue down Biscuits's ear before pressing the split halves together. The rottie's upper canines are busted to the gumline but he sports an enormous erection.

Alison swabs Matilda's nose with adrenaline chloride 1:1000 to jack some energy into her through the mucous membranes. When I remove the muzzle she nips at my hand.

Both dogs toe the scratch. The bell rings.

Biscuits slinks forward like a cat, protecting his gut. Matilda circles right, her bloodied flank resembling a port wine stain. The rottie cocks his head and goes for Matilda's throat. With blinding speed Matilda dodges back, the rottie's jaws snapping closed over vacant air, and counter-attacks. Biscuits howls as Matilda's teeth open huge wounds on the right side of his face, skin folding down in a single flap, high cheek to jowl.

"Yes!" I holler. "Get him! Get *at* him!"

Matilda presses the retreating rottie, who is blinking to clear his blood-blind eyes; spectators at pen-side shield themselves from the flying blood. She hammers her head into Biscuits's chest and flews. The rottie casts his eyes around like a lost child.

"Eat him *up*, Mattie!"

Near the end of the round Biscuits worries his head inside Matilda's guard, bites into her chest, lifts the smaller dog up and smashes her to the ground. Matilda's skull snaps off the concrete and the sound of her ribs cracking is like a boot squashing a periwinkle. The bell rings.

Matilda staggers to the corner. Her left side is dented like the hull of a galleon hit by cannon fire. Blood drips in thin rills from her ears.

"She's bleeding inside," Alison says. "Those busted ribs are pressed up against . . ."

"Do what you do."

"Pick her up. Another round could—"

"Just *do* what you *do*."

"This is such bullshit. You are such bullshit."

She injects procaine into Matilda's ribs before tending to the dog's other wounds. I feel Matilda pushing against me, eager to get at Biscuits. She is in a great deal of pain, and could die shortly. All she wants to do is fight. I remember what the dog-man from whom I'd purchased my first pit bull told me: *These dogs are bred for a mean utility. They are bred to fight and live only for the fight. It's all they know.* I wonder at a life so singular of purpose, a utilitarian existence no different from that of a hammer or shovel.

"Bad inter-cranial swelling," Alison says. "Blood's leaking out her eyes."

I use the adrenaline to swab Matilda's gums, her nostrils, her eyes covered with a thin film of blood and blinking uncontrollably. The dog's body strains mindlessly.

Biscuits drags himself to the scratch. His face,

which Lola has unsuccessfully attempted to glue back in place, is a gummy mess.

The bell rings. Matilda goes for the rottie's leg but something's wrong, she can't see right, misses by a mile, jaw hammering off the concrete. Biscuits sidesteps, clawing at Matilda's eyes, ripping the forehead open. Matilda's turning a drunken circle, trying to draw a bead, unable to. She's yowling, but whether in pain or frustration I can't tell.

"Stomp it, boy!" Lola's yelling. "Stomp that mutt!"

"Pick her up, Jay. She's dying in there."

"She's a deep gamer. She'll be . . ."

The rottie flanks Matilda's blind spot—Christ, she's *all* blind spot—and mounts her, massive jaws clamped over her neck. Matilda's squirming, yammering, unable to move. Her bladder lets go with a stream of blood-red piss. Biscuits pins her to the concrete and lowers his body like he's taking a shit but he's not taking a shit, that red raw rock-hard dick—

"That's it, boy!" Lola, apoplectic. "Throw that little bitch your dirty *laig!*"

. . . and it comes to you in the sleepless witching hours, a question bracing in its simplicity. Do I deserve? In the clean sane light of day such notions are so easily dispelled, but with dawn's awakening light filtering through the Venetian blinds, quartering your face into corridors of day and darkness, the question takes on looming weight. What is essentially a biological question acquires critical moral import—a question of weakness so ingrained as to exert its sway on a cellular level. And you wonder if you are capable. Can you meet the world with fists raised, moving forward, fearless? All revolves within this. Advance. Retreat. Weakness. Strength. If you are capable, then so you are deserving. If not, not. At some point we all must answer to this. At some point we must stare it down. Am I capable? Do I deserve? She sleeps beside you, the woman you love, her steady exhalations raising the bedsheets

by shallow increments, you thinking, Do I? Do I? *and then . . .*

I'm launching myself into the pen, slicing my hands open on snarled chicken-wire, tripping, stumbling, dragging myself up, calf stitches breaking open with a sick internal tear and the pain has me gagging but I throw myself at the rottie, shoulder-blocking it in the ribs and falling on top of Matilda, the crowd exploding in shocked disbelief, Matilda beneath me hot and tensed and shivering, whisper *it's okay, okay-okay-okay* and then the rottie on me, ripping at my rubber-bandy legs, at my neck, trying to get at Matilda but I turn into him, shielding my dog and Matilda licking my fingers and I look to Alison and the way she's staring at me, Christ, I haven't seen that look in years, the kind of look a guy can build on then baling hooks are out and digging into the dogs, digging into me and something explodes inside my skull, a combustive fireworks display, *boom, boom, boom,* starbursts and fractured light pinwheeling before the red curtain of my tightly shut eyelids as one pure thought loops through my fritzing, blown-apart brainpan: *so this is fatherhood.*

Life in the Flesh

Two months shy of my twenty-eighth birth-
day I beat Johnny "The Kid" Starkley to death
in Tupelo, Mississippi. A stiff right to the solar
plexus sent him to the ropes, gulping for breath. I
clubbed him a pair of overhand rights and a left
just below the ear, where the jawbone connects.
Brutal punches fired straight from the hip, subtle
as a train wreck. The Kid—an apt nickname:
sandalwood-smooth skin and clear green eyes, so
light on his feet he seemed to float above the canvas—held his left arm out, that arm trembling,
red glove bobbing like a buoy on a riotous sea.
The Kid's mouthpiece stuck to his teeth, the
insides of his lips filmed with white lather, holding his left arm out as if to say, *Please, I've had*

enough, but his body too stubborn, too disciplined, to buckle to the will of his mind. I hit him until his eyes glazed over like a dying animal's, until that arm fell away, until the ref signaled for the bell.

Starkley's death hit me hard, but at the time I wouldn't cop to it. The fight was sanctioned. Marquis of Queensbury rules—I'd done nothing *wrong!*

Started juicing on Ten High bourbon and Schlitz. Went from training five hours a day at Top Rank gym to closing out the Cyclone, the gin joint next door. I shed a sickening amount of weight, skin green and jaundiced, booze destroying the mitochondria in my guts. For a few months I didn't know sobriety: sixpack for breakfast and a flask of mescal on the nightstand, brushing my teeth with apricot brandy. I saw Starkley trapped in the ropes, mouthpiece dangling out, blood filling his eyes. And, in this persistent vision, I knew he was dying, knew I was killing him, but I didn't stop. The worst part was watching Starkley grow younger with each blow—now thirty, now twenty-five, now eighteen, finally my fists slamming into this kid, this skinny-legged, sparrow-chested child hung up between the red and blue ropes.

My manager, Moe Kundler, tried to salvage me. Stumbling back from the Cyclone I'd find AA schedules taped to the door, twelve-step brochures in the mailbox. Then Moe dropped by to find me zonked on the kitchen floor, shards of shattered bottle punched into my palms, pants filled with piss and shit. He filled a pot with water and dumped it on me. I came to sputtering, fists balled and ready to rumble. He slapped me hard and said, "Clean yourself up. I'm making the phone call."

No way could I hack detox or the nuthatch, glimpsing Starkley in those Rorschach inkblots. I gathered up the money I'd ratholed and hightailed it. Thailand was my choice on account of an uninhibited sexual politic and stern non-extradition policy. I arrived in Bangkok twenty-five years ago, and have never left.

Yesterday Moe wired he's sending a hardass. Time and distance have patched our old beefs. The kid arrives on the 9:40 Air Canada out of Vancouver. Late twenties, baggy board-shorts and a garish Hawaiian shirt, eyes dark behind over-size wraparounds. Workably broad across the shoulders and chest, bull necked, narrow waisted, and small hipped. Underslung jaw and a nose busted eastward. His acute-angled brow would give any cutman the screaming meemies: heavy layers of scar tissue rim the curves beneath each eyebrow, and I know if he tastes the long knuckle the sharp ridges of bone will tear those scars to shit.

"Roberto Curry?"

"Welcome to Bangkok."

He wipes at sweat beading his forehead. "Country this hot all over?"

"Hotter," I say. "Airport's air conditioned."

Don Muang airport sits atop an arrow-headed

promontory, the darkened city stretching out below. To the west: the meandering strip of Ko Sanh Road contoured in stark neon. To the southwest: Patpong a bright starfish, lit tendrils spreading from its central hub. Humidity's intense: like breathing through boiled wool.

The taxi traces a route down Thanburi Road, skirting the Chao Phraya river. Oil-slicked waters dotted with coastal trawlers and derelict coalships, floating communes of tin-roofed sampans. Turn onto Ko Sanh Road. Almost every building converted into guest houses, every corner has long distance telephone booths with cooling AC, cafés screen *Rush Hour II* and *Brokedown Palace* on video. Sidewalks strung with stalls trafficking in pewter flasks and teak elephants, knock-off Reeboks, bootleg DVDs. A train of Thai women dressed in garishly colored sarongs walk down the side of the road toting various bundles on their heads: firewood, guavas in large porcelain bowls, sacks of kola nuts, stalks of plantains, volcano fish, deep-fried crickets in beaten tin pans.

Their husbands walk in front of them carrying not a damn thing.

The kid pockets his sunglasses stepping from the cab. His eyelids are networked with scar tissue. So he's a bleeder.

Blood ruins some fighters. Since the deaths of Johnny Owen and the Korean Duk Koo-Kim, both of whom were blood-blinded from cut eyelids, paranoid refs and ring docs are kiboshing fights at the first sight of red. Some fighters got tough bodies but weak skin—breathe on them hard, they cut. There's nothing a guy can do about it, any more than a guy with a glass jaw can help being brittle. But if that claret keeps flowing—a bad cut above the eye, say, deep and wide and vein-severed, your fighter's heart pounding merry old hell—forget it, the fight's over even if your boy's not really hurt. But Muay Thai matches are rarely stopped on blood, and trainers are permitted certain measures—double-strength adrenaline chloride, ferric acid—to handle the most vicious cuts. Of course, all the ferric acid in the world isn't going to help with the detached retinas and crushed metacarpals, but that's come what may.

We sit in a curry stall with a dining area open to the street. Green curry for me, red for the kid, plus pints of fresh guava juice. The kid axes the juice in favor of beer.

"So," I say, "what's your record?"

"Twenty-two and three. Two losses on stoppages."

"Blood?"

"Blood."

"Lose the other on a KO?"

"TKO my third fight. Soft count to some unranked tomato can."

"Get cocky?"

"Little, maybe."

"I can see that happening."

The kid digs a chicken claw out of his mouth, grimaces, spits on the sidewalk.

"Ever watch Muay Thai?"

"Sure," he says. "Bunch of skinny guys winging at each other."

Consider telling him about the fight I watched last week, the one where the loser left with hemorrhage-thinned blood pissing from his ears. Consider telling him how Muay Thai fighters strengthen their shins by pounding sand-filled bottles against them, the sound a wooden *huk-huk-huk*, until their skin's tough as boot leather. Instead I say, "How much weight you carrying?"

"Started middleweight, climbed to light heavy."

"Any vision problems, those scars?"

"Peepers are twenty-twenty."

"What kind of condition you in? Don't bother bluffing, I'll find out."

The kid rolls up a shirt sleeve and flexes his biceps muscle, pumping the brachial vein. "And body fat less than ten percent. I'm gripped, stripped, ready to rip."

"You're sweating like a bastard."

"It's the food."

"It's the heat. You'll get used to it. Training camp's outside Chang Rai, two hours south. You'll be doing road work on jungle paths. Sweat off ten pounds the first week—your cardio'll skyrocket."

The kid finishes his beer, signals for another. "Want one, coach?"

"I don't drink."

The kid nods as if he'd anticipated this weakness in me. A local woman stops beside our table. Three-quarters legs, decent tits but hatchet faced, wearing a miniskirt exposing the lower crescents of her can. Red silk skirt and scarf, gold hoop earrings, white frosted lipstick.

"Herro, boys." To the kid: "Wha jo' name?"

"I'm Tony, hon."

She rests a hand on the kid's shoulder. "Oh, ju a stron' boy, hah?" She sits on his lap. "Ju a strong, han'some big boy, hah?"

"Watch yourself with that one."

The woman pouts at me. "Ju be quiet." She

wiggles her ass into the kid's crotch. "Ju lie me, Tony?"

"Sure," the kid says. "Me love you long time." His hands knead her thighs. "Thass ni'," the woman says.

I grab the fluttering brocade of the scarf and yank it off. "Adam's apple is a dead giveaway. Now your top-quality ladymen get it surgically shaved down so's you can barely tell. But this one here—well, she's no top quality."

The aggrieved he-she snatches the scarf back. "Ju a horr'ble ma'," she says to me. The kid shoves him-her away, beating his palms on his shorts as if they're coated in flaming oil. Got a look on his face like he ate a handful of rat turds he mistook for Raisinettes.

"Ah, Christ, no!"

"I'd be inclined to blame it on the beer goggles, kid, but you've only had two. Got to watch out for the scarfed ones."

"Why didn't you tell me before I let it bounce on my dick?"

"You didn't seem keen on listening."

"You're a real peach, coach."

An open-top Isuzu drops us off at the training camp shortly after 5 A.M. It is a fine, clean morning, the kind of morning that, as they say, makes you wish you got up early more often. A scarred dirt path leads through the trees alongside a fast-running stream. The path leads into a large dusty clearing fringed by tall palms and dotted with bamboo-and-tin Nissen huts. At the far end is a long-house. The sounds of men in training are audible through its open doors.

"Stow your gear," pointing to one of the huts, "and throw on your road kit."

The kid comes out wearing gray jogging shorts, cross-trainers, a hooded sweatshirt. I retrieve a rusted bicycle leaning against the long-house and say, "Let's go."

The kid starts out in a stiff-legged trot but, warming up, his strides lengthen, smooth out.

The path is too narrow for us to navigate side by side so I fall in behind him on the bike. Soon a skunk-tail of perspiration darkens the back of his sweatshirt as we follow the path east into the rising sun.

"Give me that shirt." The kid doffs the sweatshirt and drops it in the bike basket. At the 3K mark his chest is heaving, arms hanging from his shoulders. When the path finally rounds back to the camp he sprawls out in the dirt, sucking wind.

"Piss-poor conditioning, kid, but you got heart. Wind we can work on."

"Fucking country. Can't breathe the air."

"You'll get used to it. Get home, your lungs will feel double-size. Throw on your training kit and meet me in the gym."

"Fucking country."

He comes into the long-house wearing a pair of shorts and his ring shoes, a towel draped around his neck. The tattooed face of a dog, blue and grinning, covers one shoulder. On the other shoulder a crude imp or demon brandishes a pitchfork beneath the words *Li'l Devil*.

The long-house is equipped same as any North American boxing gym. In the ring, Khru Sucharit, the legendary Muay Thai trainer, instructs Bua, a rising fighter. Bua's eighteen and has been fighting since infancy. His body is perfectly shredded, each muscle group distinct and visible beneath rough, dusky skin. He's drilling textbook hook-kicks into punch-mitts snugged over Sucharit's hands, transferring his weight to rock the old trainer back a step with every blow.

"Know what I see?" The kid points at Bua. "Skin and bones and arms and legs."

"Then you're only looking, not seeing."

"Let me know when it's time to snatch the pebble out of your hand, sensei."

Set him off on the speed bag. Hand speed's decent, and the kid's got power: the leather bag snaps hard against its ringed-iron mooring. He starts mugging, beating a rat-a-tat rhythm on the bag, bringing one knee up and then the other, two pistons in perfect cadence, lisping, "I'm the champeen, the greatest, the king."

"Pop the bag."

The kid stalks over to a tan-colored heavy bag suspended from a crossbeam and tees off. He rips a half-dozen body shots into the two-hundred-pound bag, causing it to buck on its chain. He sways at the hip in bob-and-weave style, shouldering the bag, throwing hooks and short right hands, falling in line with its rhythm before stabbing four left hooks and following with an overhand right.

The kid forces a yawn. "Okay, boss?"

"It'll do."

After a half-hour of rope skipping and shadowboxing I tell him to stop. Brew a pot of oolong tea and pour cups with lemon. We sit on the ring apron and watch Bua run footwork combos in front of a full-length mirror.

"Moe only sends me hardasses," I say. "What's your story?"

The kid wipes his face with the towel. "Moe thinks I'm a hardass?"

"You wouldn't be here otherwise."

"Well," the kid says, "could be he thinks I don't train hard enough."

"Why would he think that?"

"No idea. I win fights."

"People think you win a fight in the ring," I tell him. "But you know where the big fights are won? Right here. In the gym and on the road."

"I know, I know." The kid's heard it all before.

"Moe says you brawl like a Viking. Says you fight with your dick instead of your head."

"He told you all this already, what you asking me for?"

I nod over at Bua. "That kid's won over a hundred fights. Started when he was thirteen, fights twenty times a year. He's not a crowd favorite—he's too smart for that. He doesn't go out to make a show. He goes out to get a job done and absorb the least punishment possible."

Bua's feet flicker across a vulcanized floormat,

body circling to the left, feinting, ducking away, back to the right. The squeak of his shoes on the rubber and his breath coming into an even rhythm. The boy's so quick he could fight in a rainstorm and stay bone dry.

"I don't know where Sucharit found him," I say. "Probably on the streets. He doesn't fight for glory. He fights for a paycheck. The boy trains hard and fights for the money because he knows, even at his age, it could all be taken away."

The kid sips tea, wipes his neck. "I don't fight for the money, exactly."

"Then why?"

"I got anger."

"At who?"

"Don't know. Everyone. Not all the time, you know, but sometimes . . . it builds up. This need to hurt, even if it means getting hurt myself. And that's okay, the way I see it, because everybody stepping into the ring knows the stakes. You accept those stakes, you accept the risk—maybe you're going to get fed. No, it's not the money. Fighting, it's like, *therapy*."

Fighters like him are the hardest to train. On one hand, he's managed to inhibit his natural instinct for survival: he understands he will get hurt, bleed, and doesn't run from it. Stifling the survival instinct—to continue fighting after being knocked down, to wipe blood out of your eyes and wade back into the fray—is a trick some fighters never master. On the other hand, his anger is dangerous: it's useless, not to mention foolish, carrying too much fury into the ring. Successful fighters learn to see their opponent as a faceless thing whose weight roughly equals their own, something vertical that must be laid horizontal. But successful fighters respect their opponents: respect their power, their stamina, their will to win. Lack of respect leads to a cocky fighter blinking up into the ring lights as the ref counts him out.

Bua completes his drills and he and Sucharit walk over to the ring. The boy's body is slick with clean, healthy sweat. He smiles. The bottom front teeth have been punched out.

"Your fighter's looking good," I tell Sucharit.

Sucharit frowns: trainers never admit the worth of their fighters, especially in their presence. "He slow," Sucharit says. "Like he eat lead." He slaps the boy's toned stomach. "Hah? You eat lead, hah?"

"I thought he looked slow," says the kid.

"When's his next fight?"

"Two wee'," Sucharit says to me. "Ban'kok."

"Tell him I say he's a weak puncher," the kid says. "Girl arms."

"He understands fine," I say. "Quit making an ass."

"Tell him I got two friends I want him to meet," the kid goes on, grinning. He holds up his right fist: "Bread." He holds up the left: "And Butter."

Sucharit puts his arm around Bua's shoulder and guides him away. "Goo' luck training."

"Why'd you say that?" I say after they've gone. "Something in the air?"

"Air's fine."

The most widespread misunderstanding surrounding the death of Johnny "The Kid" Starkley is that I killed him purposefully and maliciously because he questioned my sexuality, called me *faggot* at the weigh-in. But it had nothing to do with vengeance: I'd been trained to fight until my opponent dropped or the bell went or the ref stepped in. The bell didn't ring and Ruby Goldstein didn't step in and Starkley refused to go down so I did as I'd been trained. I didn't want to kill him. My only intent was to defeat Starkley completely, leave him lying there on the canvas. I wanted him dead *to me*, dead as a threat. Nietzsche wrote, *Every man unfolds himself in fighting*. Well, that night in Tupelo, in a ring smelling of sweat and spit and cold adrenaline, I unfolded.

My popularity skyrocketed after the fight. Everyone wanted to ink the "sanctioned murderer" to their card. But by then all the fight had drained out of me. I stared at myself in every passing mirror: nose busted so many times over it couldn't rightly be called a nose anymore, right eyelid hanging half-masted due to nerve damage, cheeks so scarred they looked like carnival taffy. I understood the same thing could've happened to Starkley in a bar or back alley for no payday at all. It's just, that way it wouldn't have been on my conscience. I started juicing hard, haunting the Cyclone with the washups and fight bums, stripping down everything I'd built.

My second week in Bangkok I drifted into the Royal Jubilee Palace arena, drawn by crowd buzz and frantic ocarina music, to see my first Muay Thai match. I was mesmerized by the pre-fight rituals, the lean tan bodies, the thrill of men in close combat. The *pureness* of it all. I knew then I'd never escape. Marvin Hagler spoke for all of us when he said, *If they cut my head open, they would find one big boxing glove. That's all I am. I live it.* You can't outrun this life. Sounds weak, I know, but it's the truth. Whether it was bred into me or whether I'd always harbored the bent has long ceased to matter.

This morning I'm watching the kid shadowbox in a wash of hot, dusty sunlight pouring through slats in the long-house roof. The kid's a bully: in sparring sessions he'll remind you of a vintage Foreman, shoving his partner around before tagging him with jabs, then a hook to the body, finishing with an uppercut flush on the knockout button. Shots so hard the other guy's eyes fog despite the headgear and oversize gloves.

Problem is he can't leave his fight in the ring. Type of alpha male who'll walk into a bar and knock the bouncer's teeth out to prove he's the toughest bastard in the place. He's got serious heart: takes sparring shots so wicked they'd cripple a bear, eats up mile after mile of road like he's starving, punches a dent in the heavy bag. But there's too much of the animal in him.

The kid's sharing the ring with Bua, shadow-boxing. Sucharit's in with his boy, pointing up, down, to the side, Bua following Sucharit's pointing finger with a punch, kick, or sweep. The kid's working the opposite corner, wearing ring shoes, red trunks, and wrist wraps, flashing hard combos—double-up jab, feint, hook, hook, straight right, bob back, jab-jab, uppercut—exhaling short puffs with each punch.

"Hey, Boo-boo." He's taken to calling Bua "Boo-boo" or "Boo-hoo." Sometimes he'll creep up behind the boy and holler, *Boo!* "Why don't we go a few rounds?"

"Take a break," I call from the apron. "Don't have to be a prick every day of your life."

The kid dances across the canvas, peppering jabs at Bua's back, coming within inches.

"Come on, Boo-boo, show me what you got."

I say, "Back off. *Now.*"

"What's the matter?" Dancing on the balls of his feet, shuffle-step, pittypat jab-jab-jab. "Is Boo-hoo scared? Boo-hoo a puss?"

Bua doesn't reply, eyes never leaving Sucharit's moving finger. I slide between the ropes and push the kid away. "The hell's your problem?"

He brushes past me and shoves Bua between the shoulder blades. "Let's do this. Let's do it *up*, baby."

I hook my fingers inside his trunks but, as he's a legit light heavyweight and I never fought past welterweight, I can't haul him away. "Keep this up and you're on the next steamer home."

Bua turns to face the kid. Nothing in his eyes speaks to anger—still smiling that gap-toothed smile—but his arms hang loose and ready, thigh muscles fluttering.

Sucharit steps between the fighters. "You wan' fie my boy, hah?" he says to the kid.

"What was your first clue?"

"He fie you, okay, okay. Baa no' here."

"Why not?"

"Who watch? Who *pay*?"

"Over here it isn't about who's swinging the

biggest dick," I say. "The boy's not gonna fight, nobody's paying."

"Cool." The kid's throwing jabs that stop inches from Bua's unblinking eyes. "Make a few bucks kicking his ass."

"When were you thinking?" I say to Sucharit.

"Nex' wee'. Ban'kok."

"We're gonna get it *on*, 'cause we don't get a-*long!*"

The kid raises his arms and dances in the center of the ring like Ali.

A prizefighter is a freak. He's got maybe ten years in the roughest business in the world, a business ruled by a strict hierarchy: winners and losers. He's not a paperhanger, a lawyer, a beancounter. He doesn't put on his galoshes, grab his briefcase, catch the trolley, the same daily grind for thirty, forty years. He gives it all now, or never.

Moe Kundler told me that. Moe was a fighter himself, cruiser-weight, never held a belt or scored a big payday, a crippling right hook but a weak chin led to three consecutive canvas naps and eliminated him as a contender. The ring turns fighters into freaks by aging them prematurely: that twenty-two-square-foot expanse is a time warp.

The Royal Jubilee Palace arena's prep area is located in the building's bowels. Me and the kid in a shoebox-sized room, low ceiling, pipes rattling overhead. Six or seven shattered chicken coops in one corner, floor crusted with plaster flakes and dead roaches. Above, the dim babble of the crowd cheering the semi-main.

I called Moe and asked was it okay the kid fought Bua. I said, "The only way this kid's going to progress is to take a rude beating. Only way he'll learn." Moe was wary when he heard it was a mixed-discipline bout, Muay Thai versus boxing. "Will his record be affected?" I said no, since the fight wasn't sanctioned. Moe said, "So the other guy can kick?" I said *yes*, and headbutt, and elbow. Moe said, "Could the kid get hurt bad?"

I said, "A chance. What he needs." Moe said, "Then go for it."

The kid's perched on the edge of a prep table. I'm taping his hands. Wrap adhesive gauze around his wrists to protect the eight interlocking carpal bones, across the meat of his palms, his thumbs, fingers to the second knuckle. The wrap's got to be tight, but not too tight: a fighter with blue hands is bound to break bones and not even know it.

"Flex your fingers," I say. The kid curls his hands into tight fists. "Okay. Now the gloves."

I help him on with the gloves—ten ouncers instead of WBA-sanctioned sixteens—and tape them to his wrists. The kid hops off the table, high-stepping, rolling his shoulders loose. Then the sweat comes and he's shadowboxing, holding his gloves up, juking his head to the right of them, to the left, cracking hard jabs from the guard.

"Stand back in your stance," I tell him. "Otherwise he'll kick your thighs into ground chuck."

The kid's dressed Tyson chic: black trunks, black ring shoes, no socks or robe, just a black terry-cloth towel with a hole cut in the center to pass his head.

"Remember your elbows," I say. "Legal in Muay Thai. Headbutts, too." Like every pro fighter, the kid's been taught how to fire elbows and butt heads. Only this time he doesn't have to worry about the DQ.

"For the thousands in attendance, and the millions watching around the globe," he intones, slamming his fists together. "Let's get ready to rum-*buuuuul!*"

The kid looks pale under the hot ring lights, skin glowing against his dark trappings. Bua's wearing green trunks fringed with gold, yellow shoes, the traditional Muay Thai headpiece of braided hemp. Although the kid outweighs him by twenty pounds, Bua's arms and legs are long, rangy, his hands huge—*tack hammers*, Moe'd call them. Judging by the stare-down it seems probable one or both will leave the ring on a stretcher.

The Royal Jubilee Palace—nicknamed "The Pail"—is a three-tiered arena: its levels, instead of extending outwards, are stacked one atop another, giving fighters the impression they're fighting at the bottom of a bucket. Ten-foot-high chicken-wire barriers ring each tier to discourage fans from hurling Singha beer bottles and other trash into the ring. The place is rife with chattering voices, like a forest full of monkeys.

I water the kid, grease his cheeks and brows, remove his mouthpiece from the ice bucket and slip it into his mouth. Sucharit is massaging Bua's shoulders and whispering in his ear. The ref, a tiny balding Thai in a sweat-stained zebra get-up, calls the fighters together, makes them touch gloves. The ocarina quartet place their lips to their wide-bellied instruments. The bell rings.

The kid rushes out, gloves held over his mouth, elbows out, head down, looking at Bua out of the tops of his eyes. Bua circles out of his corner to the left, standing high on his toes, hands low, wrists rotating. They meet near the ropes, Bua stabbing two quick jabs.

The kid takes the first one high on the forehead. The second one he slips over his left shoulder and, stepping in with his right foot, brings his left hand up in a tight arc. The uppercut catches Bua on the throat under his chin. His legs jelly a little. Kid goes low, knees flexing, fires another submarine shot. Bua grabs him, pulling their bodies flush. The kid's gloves are high on Bua's chest but he can't push him off. He brings them up into the boy's face, rubbing the laces across the cheeks and eyes. He's looking to the ref for a break.

"No breaks!" I holler over the crowd noise. "Fight out! Fight *out!*"

Bua brings his left knee up into the kid's side beneath the kidney. The kid lets out a grunt. Bua knees him again, putting all his weight into it. The crowd rises to a quick roar. In close, the kid shoves against Bua's face, gets some separation and brings an elbow up into the gap, shearing it across Bua's chin. Bua reels into the ring's center.

The kid comes on, stance switched to south-paw. He jabs once, twice, again, setting up the overhand right. Bua's still groggy, stepping to his left with the left foot and throwing a left hook over the jab. The kid turns under it and, as he takes the punch above the ear, fires his own right return into the short rib, carrying his weight onto the left foot, ripping another hard right into the same spot.

Bua fires a side-kick into the kid's thigh, the sound of meat on meat a bullwhip's crack. The kid staggers but Bua overbalances, too much weight on the back right leg, and the kid recovers to step in low, rising with a powerful right cross.

The boy goes down. He goes down on his butt and the back of his head hits the canvas.

The crowd becomes very still. The ocarina musicians, whose playing had risen to a fever pitch, cease. The boy rises to his knees, gloves

pressed to the canvas. Shaking his head violently,
shaking the cobwebs off.

"... t'ree ... fo' ..."

He reaches for the rope and pulls himself up.
Still shaking his head. The kid's standing in a
neutral corner, mugging to the crowd. "It's all
over but the crying, coach," he says. But it's not.
If he knew anything about anything, he'd know
that.

"... si' ... seben ..."

The kid can crack; that cross would've crum-
bled most fighters in his weight class. But Bua's
up by the ref's count of eight. His face is red and
glove burned.

The kid charges out of the neutral corner
throwing a right-lead haymaker aimed to take the
boy's head off. Bua ducks low and brings a sharp
left up into the stomach. The kid caves at the
waist and grunts in pain. Swiveling to the outside,
Bua vises his arms on either side of his opponent's
head and, thrusting forward, drives first the left
knee, then the right, into his gut.

The kid's tough. But the boy *lives* tough. The kid fights to remind himself he's still breathing. The boy thinks about enduring, surviving. They haven't grown up the same: one has never gone hungry, never watched a man die or fought for his life. All this matters in the ring.

Bua steps back and, as the kid straightens himself, attacks the right leg with three roundhouse kicks. The kid gasps. His knee buckles. Bua feints another roundhouse and, when the kid drops his guard hand, sets both feet and leaps, right arm cocked like a pistol's hammer, fist smashing into the kid's face, opening a deep gash over the eyebrow.

Not knowing what to do, the kid bear hugs Bua, tying his arms up. Blood's pissing out the side of his face and he's spat the mouthpiece. They butt foreheads and, like magic, the other eyebrow opens up. The kid's squirting blood all over the damn place.

They break the clinch. The kid must be seeing black from the blood: he's wiping at both eyes to clear his vision. He's seeing only the outline of Bua, dark arms and legs. He's backing away, staring around at nothing. Now he moves forward, but uncertainly, no strength or conviction in his movements. It happens very quickly.

Planting his left foot on the canvas, Bua pivots forward on his heel. His right arm uncurls like a whip as it comes around, arcing up, a textbook spinning backfist that hits the kid on the left temple and he goes down, eyes closing. He hits the canvas open mouthed—I hear his teeth click shut. The referee kneels, counting, the kid's body lying there, writhing, trying to get up, unwilling to surrender consciousness.

". . . ni' . . . ten . . ."

At one minute and thirty-six seconds of the first round the ref signals for the bell.

The boy walks to his corner and sits on a stool. Sucharit removes the mouthpiece and waters him, smoothing an iced metal swell-stop over the mouse on his forehead. The crowd chants his name but he doesn't acknowledge them. His face shows no emotion. He looks so old.

Helped by two attendants, I get the kid down to the training room. Crack a smelling salt and wave it under his nose. Five seconds later he regains consciousness and sits up on the table. He stares at me with cloudy blue eyes, face sweat-stung and flecked with dried blood. I flush the cuts with hydrogen peroxide, press split meat together and apply butterfly bandages, make him swallow a few vitamin K tablets.

"You came out like a house on fire," I tell him. "Had him dazed but went for too much too soon."

I cut the tape and pull the gloves off. The kid looks at his hands, at his legs, hands again, up at the ceiling. As if he has no idea where he is, as if he cannot quite believe he's here. Quiet in the room, just the kid breathing. His eyes are unfocused and he raises his left hand in front of them, that hand shivering a little.

"You'll rebound from this," I say. "Maybe the best thing for you."

The kid shoots me a look. Feral, that look. *Cold.* He lowers his hand to his lap. His index finger points at the floor. I look where his finger is pointing, thinking I should call the doctor because nothing's on the floor, the floor is bare—

I never see the dummy right uppercut that catches me flush on the knockout button. My legs crumple beneath me and blackness pours in.

I come to sometime later. The kid's gone. So is my wallet and training kit. Don't know how long I've been out because my watch is missing. Upper lip split to the septum and jaw not working properly. I don't know what to do. A lot of blood. Pick myself up and walk out to the street.

The city is alien in a way I've never known. Small torn-eared dogs fight over knots of gristle flung behind a curry stall. A figure passes whose sex I cannot determine; he or she smells of cocoa and lemon-grass and something else and carries a small colored parcel. I lean on the wall of the Royal Jubilee Palace beneath a scrawl of graffiti, a battle cry or revolutionary slogan. Blood soaks the front of my shirt and something is broken on the left side of my face. From an open window of a nearby tenement I hear the last notes of "Let It Be," by the Beatles. A shoeless boy stares at the old *farang* shivering in the heat.

The night Starkley died, a writer of no small eminence eulogized: *As he took those eighteen punches something happened to everyone within psychic range of the event. Some part of his death reached out to us. One felt it hover in the air. He was still standing in the ropes, trapped as he had been before, he gave some little half smile of regret, as if he were saying, "I didn't know I was going to die just yet," and then, his head leaning back but still erect, his death came to breathe around him.* None of this happened, though somehow I wish it had. Nothing reached out. I saw no smile, regretful or otherwise. Starkley's mouth was slack, mouthpiece hanging halfway out, saliva-stuck to his upper teeth on the left side, eyes rolled back in his skull. I didn't feel his death breathe around me. He died twelve hours later at Cedars-Sinai of a ruptured blood vessel in his brain. He'd been clear-headed, chatty I'm told, until, complaining of a little headache, he lay down and never got back up. It was an accident. It happens.

But, those last few punches—I knew something very ugly was happening. I was fully aware. I see it all so clearly now. His left arm held out, trembling, *Please*. My arm swiveling smoothly in its shoulder socket, the pressure of his face against my gloves, the shockwave coursing through the bones of my fingers, wrist, arm—I *feel* it to this day. And it felt good. Christ, it sickens me to say, but there it is. *Good*. Where did it come from, that urge? Starkley never did a thing wrong. He was a fair fighter. A professional. In the training room afterwards, Moe said, "Those uppercuts you landed near the end . . . the

Kid couldn't protect himself." I said, "I know." Moe said quietly, "I think you mighta killed him." I said, "I think so." The fact Starkley stayed up gave me all the license I needed. Why wouldn't he just *go down?* It seemed so strange. Why did he give me the chance? I never wanted that chance.

To my left the mouth of a narrow alleyway runs between the arena and the burnt-out building beside it. The brick of the building is charred and words are scratched into the blackness. In the alleyway's dim light men ring an oildrum fire, passing a bottle of Mekong. They are laughing and I wonder at what. One reaches across the flames to touch another's laughing face.